The Scorching Vessel

Solaceum Saga: Book One

AF515873

By A.M. ISMAIL

The Scorching Vessel
Solaceum Saga: Book One

Copyright © 2025 A.M. ISMAIL
All rights reserved.

No part of this book may be reproduced, stored in a retrieval system, or transmitted in any form or by any means—electronic, mechanical, photocopying, recording, or otherwise—without prior written permission of the author, except for brief quotations used in reviews or critical articles.

This is a work of fiction. Names, characters, places, and events are products of the author's imagination or are used fictitiously. Any resemblance to actual persons, living or dead, or real events is purely coincidental.

First Edition

Published by MOHAMMED ISMAIL A

ISBN (Paperback): 978-93-344-2563-5

Cover design and artwork created by the author with AI assistance.

To every soul who carries a spark of hope through
the darkest nights—
may your flame never falter.

Table of Contents

The Solaceum Flame: Origins

Before the first dawn, the Primordial Darkness hungered over a silent void—until the Solaceum Flame rose, not to conquer, but to protect. Its light breathed the world into being and stands yet as pure will: so long as the Flame endures, darkness cannot wholly prevail.

The Solaceum chose a mortal vessel—the First Flamebearer—to be protector, commander, and the keystone between light and shadow. From that vow grew the Arethean Circle, oathbound guardians gifted a fraction of the light to sense corruption, stand the line, and shield the Bearer across generations.

But envy seeded betrayal. From the Circle's fallen arose the Black Seal Order, sworn to the void, wielding shadowcraft and summoning horrors beyond the Veil. Their purpose is singular: break the

Bearer, unhouse the Flame, and usher a night without dawn.

To spare the innocent, the Veil of Solaceum conceals this war. Most know only rumors and old cautions; the Circle keeps watch from hidden sanctums, erasing traces where it must, holding wards where they can still sing.

When a Bearer falls, the Flame cannot linger vessel-less; it weakens, flickers, and seeks a heart not of strength alone, but of selfless will. If no vessel answers, the light gutters—and hope with it.

This story begins when the Flame chooses where no one expects.

Chapter 1: The Dying Flame

The air over the Ruins of Solareign shimmered with the heat of late summer, the stones baking beneath the relentless sun. Below the ridge, Stonehaven's lime-dusted lanes dozed in the noon light, close enough for the bell to carry, far enough to leave him to the stones. Lucian Calder leaned against his hammer and wiped the sweat from his brow with a dust-stained sleeve. The hammer had been his father's—war-issue iron turned to a mason's trade after the border took the man and left the tool. Dust clung to his hair, his tunic, his calloused hands—the kind of honest grime earned from shaping stone since boyhood.

His fellow masons joked that the old ruins were cursed, that their forefathers had abandoned them for a reason. Lucian felt no curse, only the wear of forgotten time. He enjoyed the solitude here, away from noisy villagers. Since his mother's sickness carried her off last winter, the ruins' quiet suited him better than the cottage's empty window in Stonehaven. The half-collapsed archways and shattered glyph-stones spoke a silent language, one he sometimes thought he could almost understand.

Today, he had lingered longer than usual. Most of the crew had returned to the village hours ago, but Lucian often stayed late to finish what he started. He was shaping a block to repair a cracked foundation line when the wind turned suddenly cold. He glanced up. No clouds, no storm. But the light itself dimmed, like dusk creeping in out of season.

And then he felt it—a rolling tremor deep in the earth, faint but insistent, as though some vast heartbeat had faltered.

He rose carefully. Picked up the hammer, not as a tool now, but a possible weapon.

From behind a broken wall came the sound of stone dragging on stone, then a low, ragged breath. Lucian's heart seized. He edged toward the sound, every instinct screaming to flee back to the village.

But curiosity—or perhaps stubborn duty—carried him forward.

At the shadowed base of a fallen pillar lay a man. No... not merely a man. He looked half-consumed by firelight from within, glowing veins running through torn flesh. His armor was scorched, emblazoned with sigils unfamiliar to Lucian, as if sunfire itself had been captured and etched in steel. His once-golden cloak, now blackened at the edges, was soaked with blood.

The figure turned his head slowly, his eyes fading embers. "You there... mortal stone-shaper... come closer."

Lucian froze. No villager spoke in such tones, each word dense with gravity. His hammer trembled in his hand. "You... you need help."

The man gave a rasping laugh. "Help I cannot have. Only a flame to give... before it is lost."

Lucian knelt despite himself. He had seen men die before—crushed under quarry rock, swallowed by sickness—but never anything like this. Heat radiated painfully from the stranger, though his flesh seemed ready to collapse.

"What happened to you?"

"Battle," the man whispered. "Betrayal... shadows unending. I am Seraphis—the Flamebearer. Guardian of Solaceum. Its fire... leaves me. It must endure, or all the world breaks."

Lucian shook his head, not understanding, but instinct told him the man's words mattered like none he'd heard before. "Save your strength. I can fetch a healer."

Seraphis coughed, firelight spilling between his lips. "No healer can bind light. Only vessel. The Flame searches, and I... am ending." His hand, scorched but steady, gripped Lucian's shirt with impossible strength. "You carried burdens not yours. That is why it calls."

Before Lucian could speak or pull away, the man's chest blazed. A searing brilliance burst forth, brighter than the sun's eye. Lucian cried out, throwing up his arms—but the light ignored defense, sinking into him like molten iron poured into a mold.

Agony unlike any he had ever known consumed him. His veins ignited. His lungs felt seared. He staggered, screaming. Fire engulfed his hands, his arms, his whole being, yet his body did not crumble to ash. His hammer clattered from his grasp.

Through the roar of the inferno in his blood, he heard Seraphis gasp a final word:

“Bear it... or all falls to darkness...”

And then silence.

Lucian collapsed to his knees, body convulsing. The crackle of fire came from nowhere and everywhere—torches flaring in the ruin, stone emitting embers, his own breath steaming like smoke. He slammed his hands to the ground, trying to claw the burning out of himself. But each heartbeat only intensified the blaze.

Then another sound rose—shrieks, low and guttural. From the crumbling arches emerged twisted forms, shadows given shape. Thin limbs, elongated claws, eyes empty voids.

Lucian’s first thought wasn’t a name but a

childhood whisper—Stonehaven gossips trading tales of 'shadow-things' that prowled old roads, stories the elders waved off for scaring children. Legend had never said what they looked like up close. Now he knew—only he still didn't have a word for them.

Their wailing pierced the still air, and some stubborn part of him still tried to call them tricks of light, as the elders did.

Lucian staggered upright. His hammer was gone, but his hands burned like brands. The creatures surged forward. He held up his hand in raw instinct—and fire roared.

The blast was wild, uncontrolled, a torrent of molten fury. It engulfed the leading beast, reducing it to scorched fragments, but the backrush flung Lucian tumbling. He smashed against stone, coughing as heat rolled off him uncontrollably. Another surge rippled, shooting a jet sideways into a ruined wall, collapsing it in rubble.

The creatures hissed and recoiled. They circled warily, some darting in, swiping with claws that passed just short as Lucian lashed about in panicked bursts. One false step, and his body convulsed, flame screaming outward. He was weapon and hazard both.

Finally, eyes blazing with terror and desperation, he thrust both arms forward. A pillar of fire erupted, searing half the pack to ashes. The others fled, shrieking back into shadow. The ruins fell silent once more, save for Lucian's ragged breaths.

He collapsed to hands and knees. The fire inside dimmed to embers but lingered, seething under his skin. His vision swam. He realized dimly he had just killed, and nearly destroyed himself in doing so.

Nearby, Seraphis's body dissolved. Not rotting, but turning to pure light ash, scattering in the warm wind. A cloak fell, charred but intact, emblazoned with the same sun-sigil Lucian had glimpsed before. He reached for it with shaking hands, clutching it to his chest without understanding why.

Bear it... or all falls to darkness.

As the sun slipped behind the hills, Lucian staggered from the ruins, fire flickering faint around his shoulders. His every step left a faint scorch on the stone. He knew nothing of what he had just inherited—only that his life, and perhaps all lives, had been set alight.

And in the gathering distance, unseen, a cloaked man mounted on a black steed watched the rising glow. His face hidden, his smile cruel.

“The new flame stirs,” muttered Kaelen Duskbane, his voice a serpent’s hiss. “Let’s see how long before it gutters.”

The hunt had begun.

Chapter 2: Fugitive of Fire

The next morning dawned pale, yet to Lucian it felt more blinding than midday. His skin tingled as if frostbitten, though heat simmered beneath every breath. He had not slept. Through the long hours he had drifted between fire-fueled fever dreams and a prickling awareness of torch-like light coursing through his veins.

He had stumbled back home in the night, clutching Seraphis's cloak, too shaken to speak with anyone. The cloak now lay folded on his straw bed, shimmering faintly in the half-light of dawn. He sat by the window, clutching a mug of water that tasted of smoke no matter how often he rinsed it.

His cottage was small—little more than stacked stones and timber beams, with shutters that creaked and groaned. It faced the mill lane of Stonehaven, where his mother used to lean in the window and wave him in for thyme tea; now the shutter was shut against dust and memory alike. To him, it had always been enough. But now the walls felt frail, too thin to contain the boiling light he carried in his chest.

Lucian pressed his palms against his knees, focusing on steady breaths. But each exhale released faint wisps of ember. His heart pounded. Each thud felt molten.

What has happened to me?

Outside, the village stirred. Children's voices rang faintly, carts creaked along the dirt road. Familiar sounds—grounding sounds. Yet when Lucian heard them now, a spike of fear pierced him. What if the fire bursts again? What if I burn them like stone?

A knock came against his door. He stiffened. "Lucian? You still in there?" It was Thom, one of the other masons.

Lucian swallowed, throat dry. "Aye, here. Just... not feeling right."

"You looked like you'd seen death yesterday," Thom said, jovial tone edged with concern. "Want me to fetch the healer?"

"No!" Lucian barked. Too fast, too loud. He steadied his voice. "No. I'll manage."

Silence hung. Finally Thom muttered, "Well, be sure you do. Everyone's talking. Said they saw flashes over the ruin. Flames. Some think you lit a forge out there. Others..." His words faltered. "... Others say darker things."

The knock retreated. Lucian exhaled, heartbeat hammering. He could not stay. The whispers would grow, fear would spread. He had lived here all his life, trusted among neighbors, but one slip of flame could end it all.

His gaze fell to the cloak on the bed. Seraphis's words returned, heavy as stone: Bear it... or all falls to darkness.

Lucian stood. He donned a rough traveling tunic, slung a satchel, and with trembling hands draped the scorched cloak around his shoulders. It seemed to weigh nothing yet carried presence, like mantle and burden both.

He left through the back path, slipping away before the village stirred further. The forest loomed beyond the fields—the Hollow Forest, wide and ancient, with roots that half the villagers swore were haunted. To Lucian, it was simply the direction most away from everyone else.

***

The Hollow Forest greeted him with quiet that felt alive. Towering pines and oaks knotted together, their canopy scattering the sun into shifting green light. The air was cooler, damp with moss and earth.

Here, away from eyes, Lucian dared try again. He held out his hand. The memory of last night's battle burned—terrifying, yet undeniable. Could he call the flame without destroying?

He took a breath. At once his chest ached, a furnace stirring to fullness. Heat surged down his arm, pooling in his palm. A flicker. A spark.

Then with a crack, flame burst outward, sending him stumbling. His tunic sleeve smoldered. He slapped it out, wincing.

"Not like that," he muttered. He planted his feet, clenched jaw, tried again. Heat rose—but so did fear: fear of another blast, of fire devouring him. And each time he feared, the flame grew wilder, shaking loose like a torrential river against cracked stone.

Exhausted, he dropped against a tree. Sweat rolled down his face. This will tear me apart.

Then he felt it—a chill, gnawing at the back of his neck. The same unnatural cold he'd felt before the shadow-creatures came. It came not from within, but from somewhere deeper in the forest.

Lucian rose slowly, every muscle taut. The birds had stopped chirping. The silence thickened. He turned—and saw, peering through the trees, three black shapes.

Voidspawn. Their forms were crooked, part-human part-wraith, like shadows clawed into flesh. Their eyes glowed a hungerless emptiness. And they had found him.

Lucian stumbled back. The flame surged,

sensing danger, erupting into his fists. But his fear spiked as well. Light flared uncontrolled, trees catching spark. The creatures shrieked and rushed.

He lashed out, fire exploding in a ravenous arc. One beast burned to ash, but the blast threw Lucian backward into the dirt, ribs screaming. He struggled to rise, vision wavering.

The remaining fiends circled. One leapt—only to be intercepted.

A figure in silver-etched armor crashed from the brush, blade gleaming with soft golden radiance. The warrior struck once, cleaving shadow in two. Another followed, a staff raised, chanting words like a hymn. Bright light rippled. The last Voidspawn shrieked as if dissolving under sunlight, scattering like soot on wind.

Lucian blinked, breath ragged. Two strangers stood before him.

The first was tall, broad shouldered, his armor scarred but cared for. His hair was streaked with gray, eyes hardened as steel. His sword pulsed faint light. He looked at Lucian as one measures an enemy, not an ally.

The second figure lowered her staff. She was younger—perhaps Lucian's age—with auburn hair bound neatly, her expression calm but curious. The radiance of her staff faded to a faint glow, like embers left in a hearth.

The armored man spoke, voice gruff: "You. What are you doing with that light?"

Lucian swallowed. "Lucian Calder, of Stonehaven." The words came haltingly. "I… I don't know. It wasn't my choice. The Flame—"

"... The Flame?" Suspicion sharpened the man's tone. He took a step closer. "Do not speak of the Solaceum Flame lightly, boy. That light belongs to the Bearer alone."

The woman touched his arm gently. "Eryndor. Look." She gestured toward the cloak slung over Lucian's shoulders. Her eyes softened as she recognized the sigil.

Eryndor's brows furrowed. His voice dropped, heavy with disbelief. "That cloak belonged to Seraphis."

Lucian nodded weakly. “He gave... no. He died. And the flame—it came to me.” His throat knotted. “I didn’t ask for it.”

Seliora’s breath caught. “What—my father died?”

Eryndor’s hand tightened on his blade hilt. “Blasphemy. That you, a commoner, claim to bear—”

Seliora’s voice cut gently but firmly. “The light does not lie. I see it in him. Do you not feel it, Eryndor? The Solaceum sings through him.”

Lucian stared between them, heart hammering. “If you know what this is, tell me what to do. It’s killing me.”

The woman—Seliora, he now heard her name—stepped forward, extending a hand. Her eyes held compassion, a warmth unlike anything Lucian had known since the fire entered him. “Then come with us. To the Circle. The Flame does not choose idly.”

But Eryndor’s expression remained carved from stone. “If shadows pursued him this soon, Kaelen will know. The Order will hunt. Bringing him risks all of us."

Seliora's gaze did not waver. "And abandoning him dooms more."

Eryndor clenched his jaw, muscles ticking. Then he gave a curt nod. "Fine. But if he falters, I will strike him down myself."

Lucian shivered. The fire blazed muted in his chest, neither flaring nor dimming, as if awaiting his choice. He swallowed hard and grasped Seliora's hand.

The Hollow Forest closed around them as they led him deeper, toward a fate he could neither flee nor fully grasp.

And behind them, unseen, a shadow lingered among the trees. Davrax, once-guardian turned betrayer, watched with eyes alight in void-glow. He grinned faintly. "So the new bearer crawls among sheep. Lord Kaelen will be most pleased."

Chapter 3: Shadows and Shields

The Hollow Forest grew denser as they walked, its canopy thick enough to blot out the sun. Lucian trailed between his two strange companions, every step heavy with exhaustion and the burning weight inside him.

Eryndor moved like a carved statue brought to life. His armor rang softly with each stride, never uncertain, never yielding. Seliora's presence was gentler; her staff emitted a quiet radiance that softened the dark as if holding shadows at bay.

Lucian couldn't focus on the endless roots and towering trunks. His gaze wandered to their weapons, to their poise, and always back to the cloak around his own shoulders, now heavy with importance. What if I don't belong with these people? What if they cast me aside—or kill me?

The silence pressed in until Lucian blurted, “Who exactly are you? And what are... those things that keep hunting me?”

Eryndor didn’t glance back. “Voidspawn. Born of corruption when the Black Seal Order tears rifts in the veil.

Lucian swallowed. “We only heard rumors. No one ever proved anything.”

Eryndor’s gaze stayed forward. “By design. We clean what we can and leave no proof for panic to feed. Better gossip than despair. They hunt by scent of Solaceum. Which you now carry like a beacon.”

Lucian winced. “Then I’m... damning everyone near me.”

“Yes,” Eryndor said bluntly. “That’s why your presence is dangerous.”

Seliora shot him a sharp look. “And why it is necessary. You carry the Flame now, Lucian. Whether you wished it or not. The Arethean Circle protects the Flamebearer at all costs. That is what we are sworn to."

Lucian muttered under his breath, "You make it sound noble. Feels more like a curse."

That earned him a rare flicker of expression from Eryndor: a dry, bitter smirk. "It is both."

***

By dusk, they reached a hill where forest gave way to stone terraces half-buried in ivy. A great arch, cracked but standing, crowned the hilltop. Beyond it, stairs descended underground.

"Here," Seliora murmured. "The Sanctum of Dawn."

Torchlight flickered as they descended. Cool, musty air gave way to faint warmth—not fire, but a kind of golden breath woven into the chamber stone itself. Lucian's eyes widened. The underground hall opened vast, carved pillars wrapped with glyphs glowing softly. A pool of water lay at the center, reflecting golden light from a hovering sun-crystal above.

Seliora's voice was low. "Solaceum's breath lives in these stones. It's what steadies the veil—the skin between our world and the Primordial Darkness."

At its edges stood several armored men and women, weary-faced, perhaps a dozen at most. They turned sharply at the newcomers.

"Eryndor," one said, relief mixing with suspicion. "You return. And who..." Their eyes fell on Lucian. At once murmurs rippled.

Seliora's voice rang steady. "This is Lucian Calder. The Flame chose him."

A sharp silence followed, thick as winter.

An older woman, hair silver, stepped forward. Her posture was regal though her armor bore scars of decades. "The Flame does not choose outside the Circle." Her eyes bored into Lucian. "Unless..."

"Seraphis is dead," Eryndor cut in flatly. "His cloak rests on this boy's shoulders. And the light within him blazes, whether we approve or not."

Murmurs stirred again, and heads turned toward

Seliora first. Grief crossed her face, steady and unhidden, before she lifted her chin.

The woman's face trembled, but she stood tall. "Seraphis... fallen." Others bowed their heads, grief rippling like a wave.

Lucian felt their stares shift to him—grief hardening into anger, doubt, even fear. His chest tightened until heat seeped from his skin against his will. Embers crackled faint around his sleeve. The circle of warriors tensed instantly, hands at hilts.

"Stop!" Seliora cried, stepping between. "He cannot yet control it!" She turned back to Lucian, her voice gentler. "Breathe. Do not fight it—breathe with it."

He tried. His lungs burned, but he met her gaze and forced slow draws of air. The ember glow dimmed, though the pressure lingered like a caged storm.

The silver-haired woman spoke gravely. "If he truly bears the Flame, trial must confirm it. Else every oath we hold unravels."

Lucian swallowed, throat dry. “Trial?”

The Archwarden replies, “Proof of the Solaceum’s will. Tonight.”

Eryndor adds, “If the Primordial presses from beyond, only the Bearer’s light keeps seams from widening”

***

“Come,” Seliora said, touching Lucian’s sleeve. “Food first. No one breathes well on an empty stomach.” She led him through a side corridor into a small refectory where a single pot steamed beside rough loaves.

They sat. Lucian tore bread with shaking hands; Seliora poured broth that smelled faintly of thyme. “Hear it plain,” she murmured, voice low so only he could hear. “Solaceum is the world’s bright breath—it steadies the veil, the skin between this realm and what presses from beyond. We are Aretheans, oathbound to keep that breath and the veil in tone, and to guard the one who bears it.”

Lucian swallowed, heat in his chest answering

the steam. "Then what hunts us?"

"Not beasts," she said. "Voidspawn—leakage given shape when the veil is cut." Her eyes hardened. "The Black Seal were ours once—Aretheans who broke oath for greed and turned to the void. In exchange, the Darkness granted them shadowcraft: power to command creatures like voidspawn and to shape shadow as weapon."

He stared into the bowl. "And the thing beyond the veil?"

Seliora's answer was quiet. "The Primordial Darkness. Not a face—an ancient will that abhors shape. Your light distributes its pressure. Breathe with it, and it will obey your thought." She set the cup into his hands. "Eat. Then we prove what the Flame already knows."

The trial chamber was a circular hall below the sanctum, surrounded by runes and lit by pale flame-bowls. At the center lay a dais of white stone.

Lucian stood upon it, cloaked in Seraphis's mantle. The Aretheans encircled him, chanting words of oath and flame. He felt their light pressing at him, probing, digging like fire searching marrow.

The Solaceum inside him roared in answer. Heat surged out, threatening to consume him. He gasped, clutching his chest as veins glowed bright, casting wild shadows.

Flames licked the rune walls. The Aretheans tensed, ready to cut him down if corruption burst forth. Lucian saw their blades gleam and terror spiked—which only unleashed more fire. His body convulsed with raw light.

I can't hold it. This will kill me—!

Then a calm hand grasped his arm. Seliora, standing too close, her eyes steady and fearless. "Do not fight as if it is enemy. Listen. Feel... breathe with it. My father breathed this way when the fire threatened to take him," she murmured. "In on the fear. Out on the will."

He focused on her voice. Heart pounding, his ragged breaths slowed, flame rippling with each inhale, dimming with each exhale. Slowly, light settled, steady as a hearthfire rather than a wildfire.

The chamber hushed. The silver-haired matron raised her staff. "It is true. The Solaceum abides in him. The Flame has chosen outside the Circle for the first time."

Eryndor folded his arms, still stern. "Then he will train. If he fails, fire will consume him—and us."

Lucian barely stood upright, sweat pouring. Relief and dread tangled. So I am Flamebearer. And now the world will expect me to be more than I am.

***

The night had not ended in peace.

Not an hour later a warning horn blared through the sanctum halls. Lucian jolted from restless half-sleep, flames sparking along his arms. Eryndor burst into the chamber.

"Shadows breach the wards. To arms!"

Lucian staggered up, pulling the cloak tight. He followed the Circle warriors rushing to the outer hall.

The underground gates rattled as grotesque

Voidspawn clawed through cracks of black light. Their shrieks pierced the stone. The Aretheans struck, swords glowing, staffs blazing radiance.

Lucian froze, torn between terror and duty. The Flame inside him screamed for release, but he remembered the trial—how close he came to burning all within reach.

Seliora shouted amid the chaos, "Lucian! With us!"

A beast lunged for her. Without thought, Lucian roared and flung out his hand. Fire erupted, slamming the creature back into the wall in cinders. The flame surged too far, spreading across the floor, nearly scorching another warrior. Panicked shouts erupted, but the beasts shrank from his blaze.

Guilt and fear seized him. I can't control it! I'm going to kill them!

And yet, as shadows crowded, something shifted. He sensed them—cold voids in the air, distortions like hollows in reality itself. He could feel their positions before they struck, the Flame whispering their presence.

When another lunged at Eryndor's flank, Lucian shouted, "Behind you!" and released a snap-burst of flame. The creature fell in ashes. Eryndor glanced back sharply, eyes hard, then gave a single nod before cleaving another.

The battle raged. Lucian fought in bursts—uncontrolled, dangerous, yet vital. His own flesh burned with the strain, each strike searing his chest as though branded. But one by one, the beasts fell.

Finally, the last shriek echoed and silence returned, broken only by panting and clatter of steel.

The Aretheans looked around at the scorched chamber, ruined stone, ashes everywhere—and Lucian standing amid flame scorch marks, chest heaving, eyes glowing faint like an ember.

The silver-haired matron spoke at last. "He is untrained... unstable. But he is Bearer. Without him, this night we would not stand."

Lucian swayed on his feet, dizzy. The fire inside simmered restless, hungry, never still. He realized with grim certainty: there would be no going back. He was hunted, feared, doubted—but also essential.

And somewhere beyond these walls, Kaelen's hand was moving, for Voidspawn this bold did not come wandering.

Lucian collapsed against the wall, eyes closing, whispering to himself: I must learn this... or burn alive before I can save anyone.

Chapter 4: Skeptic's Trial

The Sanctum of Dawn should have felt safe. Its high carved walls glowed faintly with runes older than memory, etched by hands that had known the Solaceum's breath for centuries. Pools of still water reflected the pillars of flame-crystals above, lending the air a sacred reverence.

But Lucian felt only the simmering weight of suspicion. Wherever he turned, Arethean warriors eyed him like a blade left too close to a child—dangerous, misused, and unearned.

He sat alone at the edge of the training courtyard, cloak drawn tight, watching others spar in pairs. They moved with economy and grace, blades shimmering faint light as they struck, staffs flaring radiance to block. They fought as those bound to purpose since birth.

Lucian clenched his fists and felt the answering burn of the Flame flare raw and unstable beneath the skin. He envied their command. His, by contrast, was chaos in flesh.

Seliora broke from the sparring circle and approached. She wore her armor lightly, staff slung against her back. "You're brooding already. Not the best of omens."

Lucian attempted a smile but it faltered. "I'm not like them. You see how they watch me. They're waiting for me to slip."

"They are afraid," Seliora said simply, seating herself beside him. "The Flame is power beyond measure. In the wrong heart, it could destroy what we protect. They fear that, not you."

Lucian looked down. "But aren't I the wrong heart? I'm just—" He stopped, catching the bitterness in his own tone. "I've shaped stone my whole life, not destiny."

Seliora's smile was soft. "Stone endures. When the quarry crumbles, you cut new lines. Perhaps the Flame saw that in you."

Before Lucian could answer, a harsh voice carried across the courtyard. “Enough coddling.”

Eryndor strode forward, scarred face like granite. His silver-edged sword clinked as he pointed it at Lucian. “If he holds the Flame, let him prove he can wield something beyond tears.”

Seliora frowned. “It has barely been days, Eryndor. He needs time to find control.”

“Shadows will not wait,” Eryndor snapped. His gaze leveled on Lucian, unyielding. “Up. To the sands. Let us see if the Flame makes you anything more than a hazard.”

***

The training circle was marked with old glyph-stone, its sand blackened in places where fire duels had scarred it. The Circle gathered, curiosity sharp as knives.

Lucian stepped onto the sands, heart pounding. He expected a sword thrust into his hand, but Eryndor only said, “No steel. Use what your precious Flame gives.”

“I can’t control—”

“That is the point.” Eryndor raised his shining blade and settled into stance. “Attack. Or burn from your own fear.”

The crowd hushed. Lucian forced himself into a ready stance, though nothing about him felt ready. His chest ached as the Flame sensed his fear, stirring hotter. He steadied breath, stretched out a hand—and fire erupted too quickly. A wild blast tore across the circle, uncontrolled.

Eryndor shifted smoothly aside, blade lifted, the fire scattering harmlessly off glowing steel. “Too slow. And blind. Again.”

Lucian’s lungs burned. He tried again. Fire flared—stronger, but still mis-aimed, sending shocks across the arena’s wards. This time Eryndor didn’t merely dodge—he struck forward, blunt edge of his sword slamming Lucian’s ribs. “A gift of flame, wasted.”

Lucian staggered, coughing. Snickers rippled from the observing warriors. Heat rose not from the fire but from humiliation. “I didn’t ask for this!” he shouted.

"And yet you bear it. And if you cannot use it, you doom us all." Eryndor's blade lowered momentarily. His voice was steel. "The Flame requires courage, not excuses. Again."

Lucian gritted his teeth, rage sparking with helplessness. The Flame surged like it heard, rising sharp. He thrust out both hands. Fire exploded in a roaring torrent, searing the circle's edge and forcing Aretheans to shield their eyes.

Eryndor stood unmoved at its heart, sword lifted defensively, radiance countering the blaze. When flame died back, he lowered the blade.

Lucian fell to his knees, chest heaving. He had poured everything—and still, he felt emptier than ever.

The gathered warriors muttered. Some shook heads. Others whispered darkly.

Seliora knelt at his side. Her voice was firm but kind. "You cannot force harmony by rage. It is not muscle. It is will."

Eryndor turned sharply away, dismissive. “This trial proves what I thought. He will kill as many allies as enemies before he ever learns. If we survive long enough for him to grow, perhaps.”

Lucian’s face burned hotter than fire. His fists clenched sand until it bled between his fingers. He bit back words, shame a knife in his throat.

***

That night the Circle gathered in council. Lucian wasn’t invited, but he hovered at the edge of the hall, listening.

The silver-haired matron, Archwarden Maerys, spoke gravely. “We are too few. “The Black Seal stokes harder each passing moon; if they learn Seraphis is dead, they’ll invade villages openly and rot the world by inches. We need a Flamebearer now more than ever—trained, shielded, and living.”

A younger warrior argued, “But he is no Arethean. No oath sworn, no lineage bound. He is raw, unstable!”

Eryndor’s voice rumbled. “I say train him. Break

him if need be, then rebuild. All else is weakness."

Seliora countered sharply, "We are not meant to break vessels of the Flame. It chose him as he is. Perhaps we should learn why."

A warrior snapped, "Easy words from Seraphis's blood."

Seliora did not flinch. "Blood or not, the Flame chose. Our task is to make that choice worth the cost."

Arguments rose. Hissed words of distrust, desperate prayers, pleas for haste. But one truth remained at their core: they could not afford to lose him—even if none believed yet he could save them.

Lucian's head spun. He pushed from the hall in silence, the echoes of their debate clawing at his soul.

He returned to the quiet chamber where Seraphis's cloak rested. He touched the scorched sun-sigil and whispered, barely a breath: "Why me? I'm no knight. Not even a fighter. If you had stayed with your true bearer, maybe we wouldn't be here."

The cloak, of course, gave no answer. Only the

Flame in his chest pulsed warm and restless, like a heart listening, waiting.

***

The following days were trial by fire.

Eryndor drilled him relentlessly, forcing him into combat exercises with flame bursts. Every failure met harsh critique, every near-success dismissed as luck.

“You hesitate,” Eryndor barked one morning after Lucian barely singed a straw dummy. “Hesitation is death. Fire demands resolve, not apology.”

“You think I want this hesitation?” Lucian snapped, fists sparking uncontrolled.

“I think you fear yourself more than you fear your enemy,” Eryndor returned coldly. “Until that changes, you are a torch waiting to burn your friends.”

At night, Seliora guided him differently—through chants of calm, focusing exercises, meditations where she had him breathe with the fire until it flickered in rhythm with his lungs. With her, the Flame sometimes softened, shimmering quietly without searing his flesh.

For a few fleeting moments, he almost believed peace was possible.

But dreams came too: burning fields, shadow-claws tearing neighbors to ash, Kaelen's cruel smile whispering false flame. He would wake in sweat, fire flickering across the chamber until Seliora rushed in to soothe him.

***

One afternoon, training was interrupted by alarm. Scouts returned bloodied—shadow creatures had been sighted edging near the Borderlands, too close to villages.

"The Order tests our defenses," Maerys declared grimly. "But shadows this near the wards? Only possible if they are faltering." Her eyes fell on Lucian. "Without the Bearer's light, they will break entirely."

The room tensed. Lucian's stomach coiled.

"You want me to face them?"

Eryndor's stare cut through him. "If you cannot burn beasts, you'll never stand against generals. Consider this your truest trial yet."

***

By dawn, Lucian stood armored for the first time—not steel, but hardened leathers laced with sigils. The cloak of Seraphis hung heavy, the sun-sigil scorched but watchful on his back.

They set out toward the border villages, a small band of Aretheans. At the edge of the Hollow Forest, smoke already rose, acrid and bitter.

Villagers fled screaming. Shadows writhed across rooftops, clawing against ward-stones marked at doors. Voidspawn leapt at screams, their claws tearing where wards weakened.

Lucian's flame surged instantly in his chest, flaring to answer. Fear clenched him, but so too did anger—anger that innocents would die shrieking.

Eryndor barked, "Now, boy! Fight—or watch

them die!"

Lucian thrust up his hands. Fire erupted in a storm. But too wild—a hut caught, flames climbing its roof. Villagers screamed anew, fear of him mingling with fear of the Voidspawn.

No, no, no! Lucian stumbled, trying to will the fire back, but his fear only made it blaze brighter.

Seliora's voice cut through: "Breathe—steady it—do not let fear rule!"

Lucian forced a shuddering breath. The fire wavered, dimming just enough to focus. Through the haze he saw a beast leaping for a child. With a yell, he released a burst—this time narrower, controlled just a fraction. The creature burned, collapsing before it struck.

The villagers gasped, torn between awe and terror.

Lucian's eyes burned with smoke and exhaustion. But for the first time, he had chosen. Just a flicker of control, but real.

Still, when the battle ended and shadows lay in ashes, he looked back on ruined huts, terrified villagers clutching one another, and shame pierced him again. He had saved lives, yes—but also proven himself a danger to those same lives.

The Aretheans regrouped. Eryndor looked him over once, eyes unreadable, then turned away. Seliora touched his arm briefly, whispering, "Every dawn is a trial. But you walked through this one."

Lucian nodded faintly, though dread coiled. Inside, the Flame pulsed restless, both a promise and a threat—a power that could bless or burn, depending on who he chose to become.

Chapter 5: Ashes of the Past

Lucian's body ached from dawn to dusk. No part of the training spared him: drills in the courtyard until his legs gave out, breathing exercises until fire burst unbidden from his nose, sparring sessions against Aretheans stronger and swifter than he could ever hope to match just yet.

Eryndor oversaw each day like a relentless stormcloud, correcting every mistake with shouts or blunt strikes, forcing Lucian to rise no matter how often he fell.

"Again," he demanded, voice as hard as steel.

Lucian stood despite trembling legs, sweat pouring, flames sparking uncontrolled along his arm. He hurled another wild burst toward the straw target. Too wide. Eryndor smacked his shoulder with a wooden blade so hard his knees buckled.

"Do you aim to kill shadows or scorch the countryside?" the veteran barked.

Lucian grit his teeth, anger and shame tightening his chest. He'll never see more than a failure. Maybe he's right.

But then, once training ended, Seliora came. She was steady, calm, guiding with a light touch rather than hammer blows.

She led him to the sanctum's inner chamber where glyphs glowed steadily. There, fire burned within braziers not as weapon but as warmth.

"Close your eyes," she would say, her voice a balm. "Breathe. Listen to the flame within you. It is not beast nor chain. It is—like breath itself. Let it flow outward, not burst."

And so for hours they would sit. He tried. Some nights sparks filled the chamber, other nights only heat shimmered faint. But for fleeting moments, Lucian felt it—the fire settling, pulsing in rhythm with his lungs.

He told her once, quietly, “You’re the only one who doesn’t look at me like a sword about to slip from its sheath.”

She smiled faintly. “Perhaps because I see not a sword, but a man. And men may wield burdens without letting burdens wield them.”

Those words planted something in him stronger than fire: hope.

***

A week passed before they were sent again into the Borderlands. Travelers had gone missing on the roads. Disappearances left no trace but ash and silence.

Lucian marched under Seraphis’s cloak, armor tight on his shoulders, among a small patrol led by Eryndor and Seliora. Every step, he felt the eyes of others judging. At night around the fire, they shifted subtly away when his hands flared with brief sparks.

On the third twilight, as red light scattered across the pines, Lucian’s chest clenched suddenly. Cold, unnatural, like void-breath trickled through his ribs.

The Flame within pulsed in alarm.

He froze. “Something’s near. I can feel it.”

The others looked sharply. Eryndor’s eyes narrowed. “Your ‘flame sense.’“

Lucian nodded, unable to explain how certainty gnawed at him. “There, past the ridge.”

Eryndor motioned the patrol. “Move.”

They found it at dusk. An entire hamlet, but silent—doors clawed open, livestock wasted, not a soul alive. And at the square... a cross of black steel, rammed into the earth. On it hung one of their own—an Arethean scout, body twisted by corruption, once proud armor now crawling with shadow-veins. His mouth parted in a soundless scream.

Seliora’s mouth tightened. “Anchors like this nail the veil in place just long enough to rip it. Villagers speak of curses. Proof burns away before dawn, and we make sure the rest is buried.”

Lucian’s stomach churned. Seliora whispered a prayer.

Eryndor's jaw clenched grim. "Davrax."

Lucian looked at him. "Who?"

"Once an Arethean. Broke oath, sought the Black Seal when the Flame spurned him. Now hunts Bearers for his new master."

As if summoned by the name, a voice rolled across the square. "Eryndor. You have grown slower in your age."

From the dark spires of a ruined chapel stepped a man clad in corrupted steel, black scars etching across his once-noble face. His eyes burned voidfire.

Davrax's lips curled. "And this must be the 'new vessel.'" His voice dripped contempt as he looked at Lucian. "A stonemason. A joke."

Lucian's pulse thundered. Flames stirred at his shoulders unbidden.

Eryndor raised his blade, light dancing along its edge. "You profane what you were. Step back into the void you serve."

Davrax unsheathed twin axes engraved with black runes, each humming with hunger. “You sound just like Seraphis. Do you know how he screamed?”

The words cleaved Lucian deeper than steel. Rage surged. His hands erupted in fire.

Seliora’s knuckles whitened on her staff, but her voice held. “You were not worthy to speak my father’s last breath.”

Davrax lunged.

***

The square transformed into chaos. Aretheans rushed forward, clashing with voidspawn erupting from alleys. Eryndor met Davrax head on, blade clanging against axe in sparks of shadow and light.

Lucian froze for a heartbeat, overwhelmed by the cacophony, until Seliora shouted, “Lucian! The villagers’ spirits are twisted—they feed the void!”

He looked. Shadows writhed out of the bodies lying cold.

Lucian's mind leapt to old market whispers of "restless dead"—but these were threads of something else, pulled like wire out of a wound. With a gasp, he thrust his hands. Fire burst, consuming one shade in ash. Another followed, searing under his blasts.

But each blast tore through his chest, scorching him inside. His vision swam. I can't hold this!

Behind him, Eryndor stumbled under Davrax's onslaught. The corrupted warrior was fast, feral, striking in twin arcs that rattled the ground. "The Flame dies with this false bearer!" Davrax bellowed, pushing Eryndor back.

Without thought, Lucian leapt in, fire exploding wild between them. Davrax sneered as flames washed harmlessly off his darkened armor. He swung an axe, hammering Lucian to the ground. Pain burst up his ribs.

"You burn yourself more than me," Davrax spat, pressing the axe down. "Pathetic."

Lucian coughed blood, flame sputtering uncontrolled. His chest screamed. His vision blurred.

Then Seliora's voice cut through: "Breathe, Lucian! Do not rage blindly!"

Her words struck through the fog. He forced one breath, then another. The fire within steadied, shifting. He drew it not as panic but as will—and with a cry, thrust a column of fire upward. It blazed pure, slamming Davrax back with enough fury to shatter his footing.

The corrupted knight snarled, cloak aflame, his armor glowing from the blast. He recoiled, shadows curling around him. "Interesting... maybe not such a joke after all. But your fire is young. When next we meet, you will beg me for the void."

With that, he vanished into black mist, retreating with the tattered spawn.

Silence fell over the ruined hamlet.

Lucian collapsed to a knee, chest raw from burning. The Aretheans gathered, silent but shaken. Eryndor stood, still stiff but... his eyes lingered on Lucian differently now.

"You interrupted like a fool," the veteran

growled. “But you bought me a breath I needed.” He paused, then added more quietly: “Perhaps you are not entirely useless.”

For Eryndor, it was nearly praise.

Seliora knelt beside Lucian, laying her glowing hand on his arm to soothe the pain. Her eyes were bright, proud. “You listened.”

Lucian managed a weary grin. “For once.”

But as the embers faded, his thoughts lingered on Davrax’s words. Seraphis screamed. The weight of what had been lost—and the shadowed future waiting—pressed heavier than ever.

Chapter 6: The Void's Lure

The hamlet smoldered for days after Davrax's retreat. Ash still choked the air, clinging bitter to Lucian's tongue, a reminder of what had been lost—and of how little he understood the Flame's true weight.

Each night since, his dreams curdled with whispers. They came not like fleeting echoes but as voices pressed against his mind.

They will never trust you. You could end them all with a thought.

Power unchained... why fear it? Why deny it?

Lucian woke dripping with sweat, fire flickering uncontrolled across his fingers until Seliora's prayers calmed him. Though he told no one of the words, he knew: the Primordial Darkness was searching, seeping.

***

By dawn the worst of the bruises eased to a deep ache. Eryndor's bandage bit firm around one rib; Seliora's light had cooled the rest. The Solaceum knit him faster than a normal man, but the fire-burns under the skin throbbed like memory of Davrax's axes.

Word came swiftly that more villages trembled under shadow. The Arethean Circle fanned out to protect the border roads. Eryndor, Seliora, and Lucian marched south, where smoke trails marred the sky above clustered rooftops.

As they crested the ridge, the sight chilled Lucian—an entire village gathering at the square, silent, unmoving. Men, women, children, all standing stiff as statues. Their eyes were black voids.

Seliora gasped. "They've been enthralled."

Then a lone rider emerged among them, his

horse black as night, his cloak trailing shadows like a living thing.

Kaelen Duskbane.

Lucian felt the Flame recoil within him, burning, as though it recognized this man as its sworn foe.

Kaelen dismounted with elegance, his movements serpentine. His pale face, handsome once, now bore veins of shadow coiling upward. His smile was cold as steel dipped in ice.

"Well," he drawled. "The Circle is not entirely dead yet. And there he is. The false beacon." His gaze fell directly on Lucian, eyes like pits of endless dark. "You burn like a candle in storm, Fragile, Flickering. Soon snuffed."

Lucian's instinct flared. His fists blazed uncontrolled, heat pulsing wild. Eryndor stepped forward with his shining blade, warning, "Kaelen. You skirt the veil too brazenly."

"Do I?" Kaelen tilted his head, shadows spilling around him. "Perhaps because your wards crumble. Each night grows shorter, and the void longer. You are dust clinging to sunset."

He lifted a hand lazily. At once the villagers turned as one, shrieking with twisted voices. Shadows tore out of their mouths, shaping into beasts.

"They're still alive!" Seliora cried. "If they die in thrall, the Darkness claims their souls entire."

The Circle launched into chaos. Eryndor's sword gleamed, cutting shadows that shrieked. Seliora's staff blazed, light sweeping across enthralled villagers, pushing void back but not breaking chains.

Lucian faltered. His fire surged, desperate to burn—but every target now had a human shape. If I unleash it, I'll kill them all.

Kaelen's voice slithered into his mind, clear as if whispered into his ear.

Why hesitate? They are already lost. One fire, one mercy kills them before endless corruption devours them. Burn them, bearer. Burn...

Lucian gripped his skull, fire bursting

uncontrolled around him. His vision blurred. He saw flames racing from his body, villagers screaming, Seliora's eyes turning from trust to horror—

"No!" he screamed aloud, dropping to his knees, fists trembling.

Through haze, Seliora's hand pressed his arm, her voice anchoring. "Lucian! Look at me. Do not listen. The Flame is yours if you breathe with it. Only yours."

Her words pierced the fog. Lucian inhaled raggedly. The whirlwind of fire slowed. He steadied, focused past terror.

He saw then—not only shadows but threads, dark strands weaving like worms into villagers' chests. Corruption... it could be burned out, not burned through.

Rising with a growl, Lucian thrust out his hand. Fire burst not in a wide arc but in a concentrated wave. Seliora's chants wove light into his flame. Together, the blaze purified, burning through shadow threads while leaving flesh untouched.

One villager staggered free, coughing. Another. More followed, collapsing in fits but alive.

Kaelen hissed softly, amused. "So the child finds teeth. Interesting." He swung his hand. Dark spears erupted from the ground, slashing across the square. Eryndor barely deflected with shield of light. Lucian countered with bursts, fire clashing shadow midair and bursting in molten sparks.

The pain seared him from inside. His body convulsed. The more he gave, the more he burned. But he clenched his jaw. Not rage, not fear. Breathe.

At last, Kaelen laughed low. "Enough for today, fledgling flame," Kaelen said, amused. "A greater war gathers—and when it breaks, the Darkness will consume the whole world."

He vanished, dragging lingering shadows into mist. The corrupted villagers collapsed, freed, gasping.

Lucian fell hard to the earth, chest seared raw. He trembled, looking at his singed hands. For once, they were steady—not wildly aflame, but flickering, tempered.

Eryndor glanced at him long, then finally said, "You did not scorch them. You chose." Seliora's hand steadied on Lucian's shoulder. "My father would have blessed that choice."

Seliora knelt beside Lucian, placing light on his wearied form. "You burned away chains. That is the Flame's true will."

Lucian looked back at the freed villagers, then up at the dark horizon where Kaelen had vanished. Fear remained, sharp as needle. But under it, one truth pulsed:

He had not been consumed. For the first time, the Flame had obeyed his will—not his fear.

And yet, the whispers lingered still. Power is mercy only if used fully. How long before you tire of half-measures?

Lucian crushed the thought with a breath. Not tonight.

Tonight, at least, he had saved lives.

Chapter 7: Bonds Forged in Fire

The village square smoldered long into the night after Kaelen's retreat. Survivors huddled in small groups, shaken by the corruption purged from them. The Aretheans worked tirelessly to tend wounds, restore wards, and prepare the freed villagers for journey to safer lands.

Lucian sat apart. His body ached, his hands cracked and scorched from channeling flame too long. Despite Seliora's healing light, raw burn-mark veins traced up his arms, a reminder of the power eating at him from within.

The villagers' fear weighed heavier. They kept a careful distance when he walked, flinching at stray sparks—but still pressed small thanks into his palms: half a loaf, a twist of salt, a refilled waterskin. A child peeked from behind her mother, lifting both hands like little wings; the mother's voice shook, but carried steady relief. "You burned the chains and saved us," she said. "Thank you." Lucian felt the heat in his chest settle into something quieter; for a moment, the weight of the Flame felt worth the pain.

When night dropped, Eryndor approached, armor battered from battle. He tossed down a cloak-skin beside Lucian. "Drink."

Lucian took it wordlessly, drinking deep of the bitter water. His voice rasped. "They'd rather I never came."

Eryndor sat heavily beside him, gazing across the darkened square. "They fear fire because fire kills indiscriminately. Torch or wildfire, no difference when it burns your home. You bear a wildfire with little leash. Fear is natural."

Lucian clenched the cloak tighter, bitterness burning. "Then maybe I shouldn't bear it at all."

Eryndor's gaze cut to him, sharp steel. "Speak clearly."

Lucian exhaled ragged. "This Flame... it's not

mine. I didn't ask for it. All it does is hurt me, hurt those near me. It would burn less if I just ran before it consumes us all."

Eryndor was silent a long moment. When he spoke, it was not harsh but low, grim. "Seraphis said almost the same when he was chosen. He begged us to take it away. Thought himself coward, thought the Flame erred. Yet he bore it until death cut him down. Power does not choose where it lands, Calder. We do not choose burden. We choose only what we do once it is ours."

Lucian met the old warrior's eyes. For once, they were not laced with contempt but memory—equal parts grief and respect. Then his voice hardened again. "Walk if you wish. But know this: if you leave the Flame behind, all who die hereafter by shadow are as much your doing as theirs."

Eryndor rose, leaving Lucian with guilt gnawing heavier than fire.

***

That night, Lucian dreamed again.

This time he stood in a vast field of ash and scorched bones. A black sun burned above, dripping shadow. Figures writhed among the bones—villagers, Aretheans, Seliora, even Eryndor—all reaching, clawing, scorched by fire from his own hands.

Kaelen stood before him, smiling thinly. "This is truth, bearer. You cannot protect. You cannot control. You will destroy, and then you will beg me for release. All flames end in ash."

Lucian woke with a ragged cry, flame bursting uncontrolled along the chamber floor, singeing walls. Seliora rushed to him, kneeling, chanting softly until the fire dimmed.

He buried his face in his hands. "I can't keep this up, Seliora. I don't want to kill everyone I care about."

Her hand touched his scorched wrist, gentle but firm. "So don't let it consume you. You walked into that square and freed those villagers, Lucian. You saw, you chose, and you burned chains without burning the bound. That was you, not chaos, not the void. You."

Lucian met her gaze, trembling. "I almost gave

in. I heard him—Kaelen's voice—inside my head, telling me to burn them all."

Seliora's eyes darkened. "The Darkness whispers to every Bearer. It seeks cracks in the soul. What matters is not that it whispers—only that you answer with refusal."

"Seraphis heard it too," Seliora said. "He taught me the counter-breath as a child. I'm teaching it to you now."

Her words steadied him. If only faintly.

***

Two days later they marched again. Scouts had gone silent near an old watchtower, and the Circle sent Eryndor, Seliora, Lucian, and three warriors north to investigate.

Along narrow forest paths silence pressed heavy. Not even birds called.

Lucian's chest clenched—the Flame whispering void ahead. "They're waiting," he murmured.

Eryndor glanced at him. “Where?”

Lucian closed his eyes, focused. The darkness within hissed cold, but through it he felt—voids to the west, pooling like rot in water. He pointed. “There.”

Eryndor nodded to the others. “Shields up.”

Minutes later, the ambush sprang. Shadows burst from the branches, shrieking. With them came armored figures, humans twisted by corruption, bearing blades black with decay. At their head rode a woman in lacquered midnight plate, visor lifted to show a face as fine-cut as a statue and just as merciless.

‘Siris Val,’ Eryndor said, voice dropping to iron. ‘Black Seal.’

Her smile was a knife. ‘The old hound still breathes. Let’s change that.’

Steel crashed. The Aretheans held the line as Lucian and Seliora fought shoulder to shoulder, flame and light braiding through the press. Siris Val moved like a storm—two-handed void blade carving arcs that chewed wards and rang Eryndor's shield to the bone.

She feinted, then broke through, heel slamming Eryndor back against stone. The void blade rose for the killing stroke. 'Bow.'

Fear whispered through Lucian: you'll lose control. Another breath rose to meet it, steady and practiced. He set the fire not as a blast, but as a line—a chisel's edge.

'No.'

Flame leapt in a tight, clean arc, a bright crescent that met the black sword on the downstroke. For a heartbeat, void and fire held; then Solaceum burned through the rot. The void blade shattered from tip to guard. Siris staggered, shock cutting her poise.

Lucian stepped in on the breath—inhale to steady, exhale to shape—and drove a spear of fire through the seam in her cuirass. The lacquer split. Void smoke screamed and then fell silent.

Siris Val looked almost puzzled, like a dancer whose music had ended too soon. 'A stonemason,' she said softly, and collapsed into ash that tried to crawl and then, under the steady glow of Lucian's hands, lay still.

The remaining corrupted scattered. Seliora's light pursued, scouring threads; the Aretheans cut the rest down.

Silence dropped heavy as the ash. Eryndor pushed to his feet, chest scorched but breathing. He picked up his sword, studied Lucian a moment longer than pride liked, and nodded once.

'You should have fled,' he said quietly. 'Instead, you chose the line and kept it true.'

The patrol gathered—shaken, alive. Lucian's arms trembled from the channeling, but his hands were steady, the flame answering his breath instead of his panic."

Silence dropped, broken only by heavy breaths.

Eryndor stood, chest scorched but alive. He retrieved his sword, then approached Lucian slowly. For once, no contempt lined his face.

“You should have fled,” he said quietly. “Instead, you stood. You shielded my life at cost of your own strength.”

Lucian swallowed, uncertain. “I... I couldn’t let you die.”

The old warrior studied him a long moment. Then he placed a calloused hand on Lucian’s shoulder. The weight was firm, approving.

“Then perhaps, Flamebearer, there is something in you after all.”

Lucian felt warmth rise not from the Solaceum but within his chest, something steadier: acceptance. Around him, the Aretheans looked at him differently—not entirely with trust, but with the first glimmers of belonging.

For the first time since inheriting the Flame, Lucian did not feel utterly alone.

Chapter 8: Whispers of Treachery

The journey back to the Sanctum of Dawn was quiet, but not grim. Word of Siris Val's fall had run ahead of them like dawn on stone. At the gates, warriors stepped forward with weary smiles and clasped forearms; hands that once hesitated now found Lucian's wrist and held fast. Not all doubt was gone—eyes still checked for sparks—but respect had taken root, and the murmurs sounded less like fear than relief that the fire had stood with them.

***

That night, the Circle convened in the Council Hall—a great, rounded chamber etched in fire-runes that glowed faint beneath braziers, their warmth tinged faint gold.

Archwarden Maerys addressed them, her silver hair catching the light. "The Black Seal no longer hides their hand. Kaelen Duskbane himself walks corrupted villages. If their darkness stretches farther, the veils may weaken irreparably."

"Let no one mistake a slain knight for a sleeping enemy—the Black Seal will spend ten to raise what one of ours may fall to stop."

"Siris Val's defeat won us breath, not safety," an Arethean warned. "They will answer harder. We cannot sit waiting."

Eryndor's gravel voice broke across the murmur. "We are dwindled too thin to charge blindly. If we hunt shadows in open ground, we risk annihilation."

Lucian shifted uneasily, the only outsider in this circle of seasoned warriors. His word held no weight. Yet Kaelen's mocking smile haunted him, his whispers still curling along his dreams. "He's planning something larger," Lucian spoke without thinking. "That attack... felt like a test."

Dozens of eyes turned on him. Some burned with skepticism, others with irritation.

"And what wisdom does a village stonemason share of war?" one warrior scoffed.

Lucian's face flushed hot. "The Flame tells me. I feel their corruption before I see it. That was not Kaelen's full strength—only probing for weakness."

Eryndor's eyes flickered his way, unreadable. Maerys studied him long, pensive. "If the Flame warns through you, then we must heed it. Shadow strengthens when unchallenged... but caution serves also. We will split patrols, but the Sanctum must hold secure."

The council broke, murmurs lingering. As Lucian rose, he saw a warrior's glare—sharper, colder than the rest. Corvane, an older Arethean whose brother had died under Seraphis's command decades past. His gaze lingered on Lucian with muttered curse: "A cursed usurper."

Lucian said nothing, but the Flame pulsed unpleasantly in his chest. Something in Corvane's eyes unsettled him—not fear, but something harder.

***

Days passed in tense routines—training, guarding, patrolling. Yet whispers grew. Food stores misplaced, watchfires inexplicably quenched, runes at the outer walls dulled without reason.

Sabotage.

And always Lucian felt cold pricks of void where no spawn appeared, fleeting but real.

One evening, he crossed the sanctum's inner corridor and found Seliora bent in prayer by the Flamepool, its waters shimmering warmth. He started to speak—but then his Flame surged, searing in warning.

Behind her, a figure lurked in the shadows.

Lucian acted without thought. He hurled fire across the chamber. A roar of light illuminated Corvane, crooked dagger drawn, black veins crawling up his arm. He staggered back, hissed, shadows clinging to him like smoke.

"Traitor," Eryndor spat, bursting through behind Lucian, sword blazing. The Circle rushed in.

Corvane sneered, voice warped by the void. "You should never have dragged the outsider in. The Flame belongs broken—its embers poured into all, not caged in one weak vessel!"

He lunged, shadow-blade crackling corruption. Lucian threw up his hands—fire shield burst wide, intercepting the strike. Sparks showered the walls. The others swarmed, subduing him with steel and radiant chains.

Breathless, Lucian stood amid the chamber, flames dimming. Whispers of distrust turned now on Corvane, restrained, snarling void curses.

Archwarden Maerys's face was grave. "Corruption festers in secret... even among us." Her eyes swept the Circle, then settled on Lucian. "You saved Seliora this night—and this Sanctum from fracture."

A hush fell over the hall as eyes shifted from Seliora to the old sun-sigil banners—her father Seraphis's legacy, alive in her gaze.

Whispers still lingered—but subdued now, edged by reluctant gratitude for Lucian's fire.

Seliora touched his shoulder warmly. “You trusted your Flame. And it trusted you.”

But Lucian’s chest still burned with unease. Corvane’s last words echoed sharp: The Flame should not be in one vessel alone

***

The dawn after Corvane’s execution, Maerys convened them once more. “The Black Seal moves openly now. Their infiltration has struck our wards, their corruption reaches villages unchecked. And their aim is plain—to slay the Bearer before his fire matures.”

Lucian stiffened as her eyes landed on him.

Eryndor’s gravel voice followed. “Then we move first, before Kaelen calls more generals to his banner.”

Seliora’s gaze found Lucian, firm yet encouraging. “This is where you choose, Flamebearer. Will you stand with us before shadows consume what’s left?”

Lucian looked between them all—warriors scarred by loss, uncertain of him still, but waiting, their eyes searching.

For the first time, he lifted his head not only with fear but resolve. "We fight. I will stand—not alone this time. But with all of you."

A hush claimed the chamber. One by one, blades touched floors and helms dipped—not in ritual alone, but in assent. 'The Solaceum did not err,' Maerys said, staff planted, voice carrying. 'We bear witness that the Flame chose—here, now, in him.' The Circle's reply was not words but the sound of steel sheathing as if on a single breath. Eryndor inclined his head the width of a blade. Seliora did not speak; she set her palm to Lucian's shoulder, and for once no one flinched at the touch.

The Circle bowed heads, recognizing not yet their perfect bearer, but a man stepping into his own choice.

Beyond the sanctuary, in the untamed Vale of Ash, Kaelen Duskbane watched runes flare in his black mirror. His smile curved cruel.

"Good. Struggle harder, little flame. Burn brighter. For the brighter you shine, the more glorious your fall will be."

Chapter 9: March into Ash

The Vale of Ash lay like a wound upon the earth. From afar, the air shimmered with gray haze, as though smoke eternally drifted without fire. Dead trees clawed into the sky, their bark crumbling, their branches sagging with rot. The soil was black glass, fissured veins glowing faintly with seeping voidlight.

Lucian stared down from the ridge beside the Circle. A dread unlike any shadow battle before gnawed at his chest. The Flame stirred uneasily, as if recognizing this place as a scar it could not heal.

Archwarden Maerys's voice was solemn. "Here Kaelen gathers strength. The wards of old falter, and the void seeps freer each century. If he awakens what sleeps beneath, our world buckles."

Lucian swallowed hard. And I'm the one who

must stop him. From stonemason to bearer of fire, the path still felt impossible. Yet when Seliora's hand brushed his cloak in silent steadiness, courage flickered.

"We move at dusk," Eryndor growled, already checking the edge of his blade. His face carried the exhaustion of years, but his stride was still sharp. "The less the enemy sees, the less reinforcements can be summoned."

***

The descent into the Vale was like stepping through the veil itself. The air tasted of iron. Whispers hung in the haze, twisted voices beckoning. Lucian felt each one tangle with the Flame inside, scratching for cracks in his resolve.

You are weaker than the last.

They will die because of you.

Burn them now and spare them suffering.

He bit down, breathing steady. Not this time.

Yet each step grew harder, fire thrumming in painful rhythm against the void.

At the valley's depths they found ruins—once a temple, now gutted into cavernous spires black with corruption. Shadows writhed across its walls like veins in flesh. And at its heart, a vast pit pulsed, breathing ash and smoke.

Kaelen stood upon the dais above it, cloak trailing black tendrils. At his side, Davrax, twin axes gleaming voidlight. Their presence alone sickened the air.

"So the Circle limps to its grave," Kaelen's voice coiled across the ruin. "And brings its half-born bearer to perish here. Fitting."

Lucian's flame flared uncontrolled, answering enemy presence. But he steadied himself. "We came to end this. No more villages. No more chains."

Kaelen's brow arched faintly amused. "Seraphis said the same. He screamed when void carved him hollow. Shall I make you hear his echoes?"

Davrax snarled, hefting axes. "Enough talk. Let

me carve the cinder from this boy's chest."

The battle broke like a storm.

***

Aretheans charged, blades and light colliding with voidspawn erupting from the pit. The air shook under shrieks and clash. Kaelen remained apart, weaving shadows that stretched like tendrils across the field, spearing toward warriors, severing ground.

Lucian met Davrax at the center. Twin axes came in furious arcs. He raised flame-wreathed arms to block—fire erupting into radiant shield, but each impact drove pain scorching through his bones.

"You think flame makes you strong?" Davrax laughed, slamming. "It hollowed me once! When it denied me, I found power truer in shadow!"

Lucian strained. The heat built like an oven in his chest, ribs splitting. "You gave up your oath," he gasped. "You abandoned them all."

Davrax's eyes glowed void. "No... I was abandoned. And soon, you will be as well."

The axes slammed down. The shield cracked. Lucian screamed, thrusting flame outward, barely warding off the killing strike. Fire and shadow blasted in shockwave across the valley.

The Circle fought on, but pressure mounted. Kaelen towered at the pit, chanting, shadows billowing. Seliora shouted across the chaos: "He's trying to awaken it! The horror beneath the ash!"

Lucian's heart thundered. The Flame urged him desperately—strike now, or fail.

Davrax lunged again. Lucian tried to counter, but heat overran him. His knees buckled. The Flame burned him, not his foe. He coughed blood, chest searing as though molten iron split his lungs.

Davrax loomed, striking aside his weak flame bursts. "You carry a fire that's killing you, boy. I carry power that only strengthens. Who truly bears the greater gift?"

Lucian collapsed, vision narrowing, fire sputtering. The Circle cried out, too pressed to aid.

The world narrowed to heat and dark—then

opened. Not his own memory, but a vision: bearers across the ages, glimpsed where the veil thinned. The battles flickered past like reels of fire and shadow—figures standing against swarms of blackness, blades and flame cutting through claw and seal. He saw them fight not without fear, but with courage burning brighter than the dark.

Seraphis's voice moved through the vision, steady as a hand on his shoulder. "They stood not to court death, but for justice—to want peace for the innocent and to keep it with their own breath. When the Flame chose you, it did not ask you to banish fear; it asked you to bear courage. Courage is not the absence of fear—it is the will to protect in spite of it."

The images slowed: hands placing a chisel on stone, setting a clean line. "Breathe the fire as you breathed at the quarry. Set the edge like a hammer on grain. Watch your thought, and the flame will obey it. In on fear. Out on will. Shape—don't shatter."

Lucian's lungs answered before doubt could—inhale, the heat gathered and held; exhale, it ran true.

Davrax raised his axes for the final cut.

Lucian's eyes flew open. Amid pain, he inhaled. Not rage, not terror—a breath. The fire shifted instantly. No longer clawing, but flowing. No longer resistance, but rhythm.

As Davrax's axes fell, Lucian rose, radiant shield blooming stronger. Flame coursed outward, precise, shaped into a blade forming along his arm.

With a cry, Lucian struck. Fire met void in searing clash. Davrax staggered back, shocked.

"You... forged it," he hissed.

Lucian advanced, each breath shaping fire steadier, flowing into blade strikes. They clashed in fury—Davrax's void axes against Lucian's first true flame-weapon, sparks of night and sun bursting.

At last, with one heaving swing, Lucian's blade of fire shattered Davrax's left axe, searing into his shoulder. Davrax staggered, shock breaking his snarl. "You—" The word unraveled into smoke. Lucian inhaled, set the edge like a chisel, and on the exhale drove the fire-blade up under the breastplate seam. Void screamed; armor buckled. For a heartbeat, Davrax stood as if defying the inevitable. Then the corruption lost its grip. The body caved, the shadow within tore free—only to burn to ash in Lucian's steady light.

Ash fell where Davrax had stood; there would be no "next time."

Lucian collapsed to one knee, exhausted but alive, fire dimmed yet not destructive. Around him, Aretheans still fought. Above, Kaelen's chant grew louder, the pit pulsing monstrous.

He had held the line—and ended the traitor the Circle once called brother.

Seliora cried, "Lucian! He'll awaken it fully if we don't stop him!"

Lucian rose trembling, flame-blade flickering at his hand. The Flame still coursed fragile, but steady for now. One choice remained: confront Kaelen at the pit, or fail everything.

And as his gaze met the abyss, a horror stirred, vast shadow limbs clawing, answering its master's call.

The final trial of the first bearer's heir had begun.

Chapter 10: The First Breath of Dawn

The earth shuddered beneath their feet. Cracks split wide as blackened ground crumbled away, revealing the abyss below. From the pit rose a monstrosity vast as cathedral spires, a being of writhing limbs, each woven from condensed shadow and bone. Its roar shook the Vale of Ash, a keening cry that split sky and soul.

Lucian staggered, fire-flame sputtering at his hand. This... this thing was never meant to walk the mortal world.

Kaelen Duskbane stood tall upon the dais, arms outstretched, shadows coiling through him like veins. "Rise, children of the First Night. Tear the world open. Devour until light itself withers!" His laughter rang hollow as the horror clawed skyward.

Aretheans scrambled into formations. Eryndor barked orders with steel voice. Seliora's voice rose in prayers, light spiraling across her staff. But their power was drops against the ocean of void spilling into existence.

Lucian's chest seized. The Solaceum blazed, screaming inside him, desperate to answer shadow in kind—but burning him raw. He dropped to his knees, coughing blood, vision swimming red.

You'll kill yourself if you unleash it all.

Better to die than let this horror consume all, another voice urged.

He bowed his head, trembling. "I can't," he rasped. "I can't do this."

The battle's roar fell away—and Seraphis's words returned as if set into the stone of his mind: "Handle the flame as you handle hard stone. You don't smash to get your shape—you set the line, place the edge, and strike true. Breathe. Set the thought, and the fire will obey it. In on fear. Out on will."

Lucian closed his eyes and inhaled. The Flame did not claw; it gathered. He exhaled, and it ran where he told it.

Lucian rose, eyes opening, no longer wild with fire but steady, blazing like coals refined. Flames shrouded him, flowing into his hands cleanly. A blade of fire formed sharp, humming with controlled radiance. His cloak of Seraphis shimmered brighter, sigil alight as if answering the dawn.

Kaelen turned, eyes narrowing. "So... the cub finally learns to unsheathe his claws."

Lucian's voice rang steady for the first time. "Not claws, Kaelen. The dawn."

***

The void horror surged forward, titanic limb sweeping down to crush the Aretheans. Warriors screamed as they raised shields too weak to withstand.

Lucian leapt. His flame surged into wings, small flickers only, but enough to carry him high. With a great cry he brought his blade down, fire carving across the shadow limb. Light and dark clashed in eruption of sparks, severing tendrils. The horror shrieked, flailing back.

The Circle cried out as hope rekindled. "The Bearer fights!"

Kaelen snarled, shadows lashing toward Lucian like spears. He spun, flame shield whirling, sparks scattering void midair. For once, his strikes did not scorch wildly. He aimed. Each cut burned threads of corruption precise. Each burst of fire landed true.

The Aretheans rallied at his side, driving spawn back. Seliora's prayers infused his flame with radiant harmony, steadying it.

Eryndor fought close, cutting through beasts. He shouted through chaos: "Burn the core, Lucian! The beast's heart anchors the summoning!"

Lucian focused. Between the horror's writhing mass pulsed a glowing knot of voidlight. The Flame within him burned to strike.

But Kaelen barred the way, cloak unfurling into wings of darkness. He landed between Lucian and the beast, grin sharp. “First, bearer. Prove yourself to me.”

Their blades clashed—shadow and flame, sparks searing air. Kaelen’s strikes came fast, too fast, each swing cruel and mocking. “Seraphis fell to me,” he hissed. “Your fire will gutter faster.”

Lucian gasped, parried desperately, fire flaring low as Kaelen pressed. Sparks rained. His arms screamed.

But then—he remembered Eryndor, saved. Seliora’s faith. Villagers freed. The weight of all who had fallen and all who prayed now for dawn.

He inhaled. With it, the fire surged not in rage, but will. His blade steadied, parried higher, burst brighter.

Kaelen snarled as the tide shifted. “Impossible!”

Lucian struck, fire flashing along the blade, searing across Kaelen’s cloak. The corrupted knight staggered, void hissing.

“Not impossible,” Lucian growled. “Chosen.”

With a final cry, he drove fire-blade deep into Kaelen's chest. But the general dissolved into shadow before killing blow, retreating with howling promise. "This is not the end, false dawn! Next time, even your fire will not cleanse what you unleash!"

Kaelen vanished. The horror roared unchecked now, thrashing. Time was gone.

Lucian turned. Eryndor cried out, "Now, Lucian! Strike its heart!"

The horror's chest flared, void pulsing. Lucian breathed once more, flame wings flaring brighter. He soared above, fire coursing his whole form, and thrust his blade downward.

Light pierced the horror's core. Fire and void clashed in explosion that shook the Vale. Blinding radiance consumed the monster, burning corruption thread by thread until nothing remained but ash scattered on the night.

Silence followed, broken only by ragged breaths of surviving Aretheans. The pit closed, sealed by fire and earth. The air cleared faintly.

Lucian landed, stumbling. Seliora steadied him, her face shining with awe. "You did it... you truly did it."

Eryndor approached, his scarred face breaking into rare grim smile. "You breathed with it. You fought as bearer—not hazard. Seraphis would have smiled to see it."

Seliora's answer was a single nod, eyes bright. "He does."

Lucian, exhausted, glanced across the Circle. Their eyes no longer whispered suspicion but hope. For the first time, they knelt in respect.

Archwarden Maerys proclaimed, her voice carrying in the Vale: "Lucian Calder, stonemason of Solareign, you are Flamebearer, Dawn's Sentinel reborn."

The Flame within pulsed—not in searing pain, but in quiet harmony, like a hearth after storm.

Lucian bowed his head, whispering to the fallen Seraphis, to himself, to all who had borne chains: "I am bearer. And I will not let the Flame fade."

But overhead the stars dimmed faintly, as if shadows yet lingered waiting. Kaelen had fled, his master's hand unseen still.

The war was not done. This was merely the first breath of dawn against endless night.

Epilogue: Embers in the Dark

The Vale of Ash lay quiet for the first time in centuries. Where once the pit had breathed with corruption, now only a charred crater smoldered faint red, as if dawn itself had burned away a piece of the Darkness.

But silence did not mean safety.

Seliora stood at the ridge, watching Lucian below. He had refused the comfort of chambers, choosing instead to sit before the last embers of the closed pit. The cloak of Seraphis draped across his shoulders, its sigil glowing faint gold in harmony with his own faint flame.

"You don't rest," she said softly, approaching.

Lucian shook his head, eyes fixed on the crater.

"When I close my eyes, I still see it. The horror. The shadows twisting villagers. Kaelen laughing." He clenched his hand, fire flickering faintly along his knuckles. "If one battle nearly broke us, how will I hold against what comes next?"

Seliora knelt beside him, gaze gentle. "Because you will not stand alone. That is what Kaelen doesn't understand. Flames burn brightest when carried from hearth to hearth. And you are not a solitary flame now. You are a dawn rising over many."

Lucian breathed out slowly, the fire dimming, settling. "Then I'll need to learn more. Not just wild bursts. If I can shape flame into shield, maybe I can shape it into blade, armor, more..."

Seliora smiled faintly. "Eryndor will be delighted to knock sense into you until you manage it."

Lucian exhaled half a laugh—the first genuine laugh he'd allowed himself since before Seraphis's death.

But far off, unseen by them, the horizon trembled.

In the Ebon Spire—a fortress of shadow beyond mortal lands—Kaelen knelt before a vast throne of bone and black fire. His body still smoked from Lucian's strike, but his voice was steady, venomous.

"The new bearer stings. He has forged weapon-fire before his time. Dangerous... but not yet beyond breaking."

A deeper voice, vast and ancient, rumbled from the throne. The Primordial Darkness itself seeped through the hall. Then bleed him. Bleed his Circle. Let him forge his strength in fire, until mercy fuses to arrogance. His heart will feed us in time.

Kaelen bowed, a smile cutting his lips. "As you will, master. Let the embers of his will become his undoing."

The shadows deepened, swallowing even the echo of his laughter.

Back at the Vale, dawn broke pale gold across blackened stone. The Aretheans gathered, battle-weary but alive. For the first time in many years, the Flame had triumphed.

And for the first time, Lucian Calder felt the fire not as curse... but as calling.

There would be no peace, not yet. But he was ready to learn. Ready to forge.

Thank You for Reading

Your journey through The Scorching Vessel means the world to me. This is just the beginning of the Solaceum Saga, and I'd love to share more with you.

If you enjoyed The Scorching Vessel, leaving a review on Amazon helps more than you know. Even a single sentence makes a difference.

By joining my Readers' Circle, you'll receive:
- Early updates on future books
- Exclusive lore and background stories from Solaceum
- Special notes and surprises for loyal readers

Sign up for free updates: subscribepage.io/Ismail_Author

Let's keep the Flame alive together.

— A.M. ISMAIL

About the Author

A.M. ISMAIL is a storyteller passionate about crafting epic fantasy worlds and thought-provoking science fiction. His stories blend imagination with depth, inviting readers into realms where courage, hope, and resilience shape destinies.

Driven by a love for mythic themes and futuristic possibilities, Ismail writes tales that not only entertain but also inspire readers to reflect on the choices that define humanity. *The Scorching Vessel* marks the beginning of the **Solaceum Saga**, an epic journey through light, shadow, and the enduring power of will.

When not writing, he explores creativity, imagination,
and self-development,
always seeking new ways to bring worlds to life.

Stay connected with the author:

Instagram : @ismail.author

Author Bio: https://www.amazon.com/author/a.m.ismail

Goodreads: https://www.goodreads.com/ismailauthor

Also By the Author

The Veil's Edge (Solaceum Saga: Book two)— Coming Soon

Wardlines fail across the borderlands, and to stop the Black Seal from turning a living city into a gate, the Flamebearer must learn the cut that heals.

Stay tuned for future releases, short stories, and bonus lore in the Readers' Circle

Scan the QR code below to join:

Or type this link in your browser:
subscribepage.io/Ismail_Author

www.ingramcontent.com/pod-product-compliance
Ingram Content Group UK Ltd.
Pitfield, Milton Keynes, MK11 3LW, UK
UKHW040036200726
13845UKWH00054B/417

9 789334 425635